Mitsuaki Iwago's WHALES

Mitsuaki Iwago

CHRONICLE BOOKS

SAN FRANCISCO

INTRODUCTION

The humpback whales in this book were photographed in the waters off southeastern Alaska, the Hawaiian Islands, and the Bonin Islands. The map at right indicates the three locations where we photographed, as well as the humpbacks' presumed migration routes. Although their definite routes are unconfirmed, we know that they travel widely throughout the Pacific Ocean. There is no other area in the Pacific that is as warm and safe as the waters of Hawaii. When the winter breeding season arrives, humpbacks migrate to Hawaii from Alaska. Come summer they return to Alaska. The same whales have been observed around Revillagigedo Island in Alaska, off the coast of Mexico, and back in Alaska. Whales also migrate from the north to the waters off the Bonin Islands in Japan.

Serious research on humpbacks began only about ten years after whale hunting was prohibited in 1966. The humpback population is estimated at less than twenty thousand. We still have a great deal to learn.

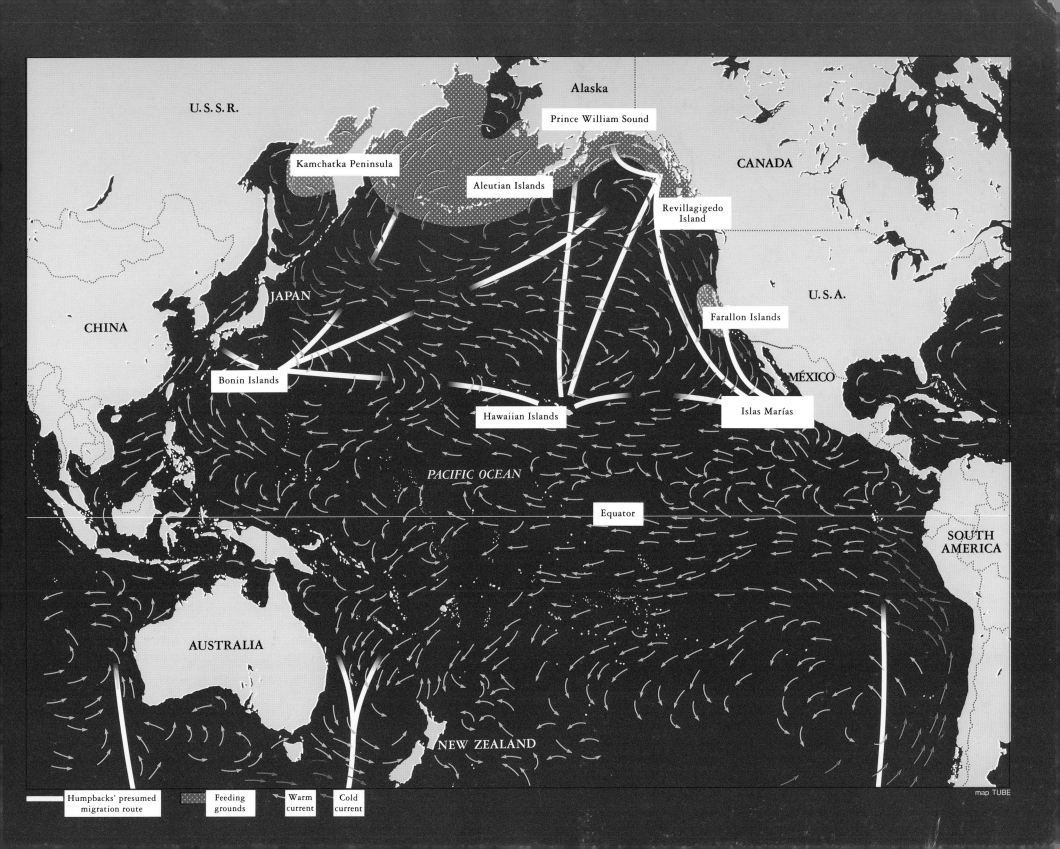

U.S.S.R.

Alaska

Prince William Sound

Kamchatka Peninsula

Aleutian Islands

Revillagigedo
Island

CANADA

JAPAN

CHINA

U.S.A.

Farallon Islands

Bonin Islands

MÉXICO

Hawaiian Islands

Islas Marías

PACIFIC OCEAN

Equator

SOUTH
AMERICA

AUSTRALIA

NEW ZEALAND

map TUBE

Humpbacks' presumed
migration route

Feeding
grounds

Warm
current

Cold
current

ON *Mitsuaki Iwago's Whales*

Mitsuaki Iwago's Whales is the product of photographer Mitsuaki Iwago's twenty-year dream to portray whales in their own element; to capture the subtle moods, complex personality, and alien marine lifestyle of this massive ocean traveler. This book is a gift of beauty. More importantly, however, it answers with poetry and grace the frequently asked question, "Why protect whales?" If a picture is worth a thousand words, then *Mitsuaki Iwago's Whales* contains an encyclopedia of reasons why the great whales must be left to continue their ageless ocean journeys, unhampered by the destructive acts of humans.

I had the good fortune to accompany Mitsuaki during part of the time he worked on this book. While photographing humpback whales in Hawaii, Alaska, and the Bonin Islands, Mitsuaki collaborated with scientists from the Pacific Whale Foundation. It was an honor and a privilege to watch him as he moved in the world of the majestic whale. With patience, poise, and a deep intuitive sense of respect for his subject, Mitsuaki Iwago has documented an extraordinary range of spectacular humpback whale behaviors, including rare photographs of their unique feeding activities, competitive courtship rituals, and care of their newborn calves. Only a few of us have witnessed intimate moments of a humpback's life; only Mitsuaki has so poignantly captured them to share with others.

As a photographer, Mitsuaki is to be congratulated for the visual banquet he lays before us. He also deserves thanks and praise as a conservationist, for reminding us of the grandeur of whales, and for increasing our resolve to ensure we do not return to the centuries of slaughter and waste that are a sorry part of our heritage. Mitsuaki leaves us with a challenge as great as the whales themselves: to treat the oceans with the grace, wisdom, and sensitivity with which he has portrayed his subject in these photographs. The beauty of this book is surpassed only by the urgency of that underlying message.

Paul H. Forestell, Ph.D.
Director of Research
Pacific Whale Foundation

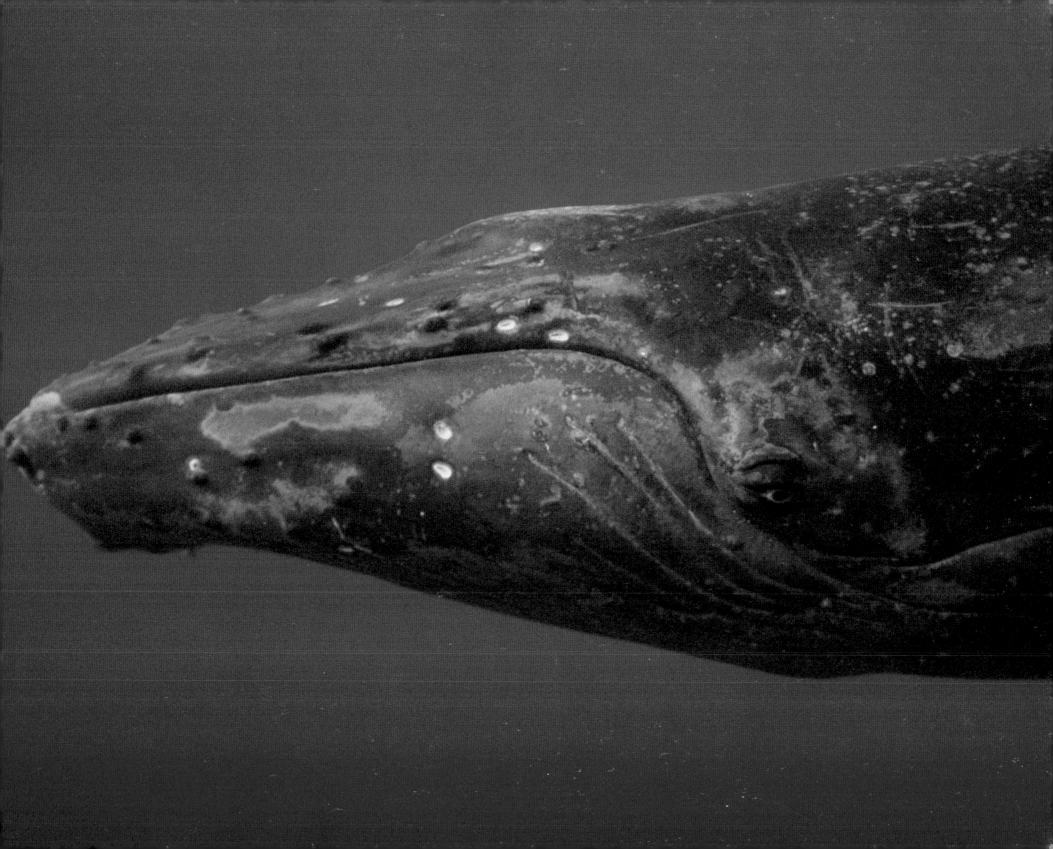

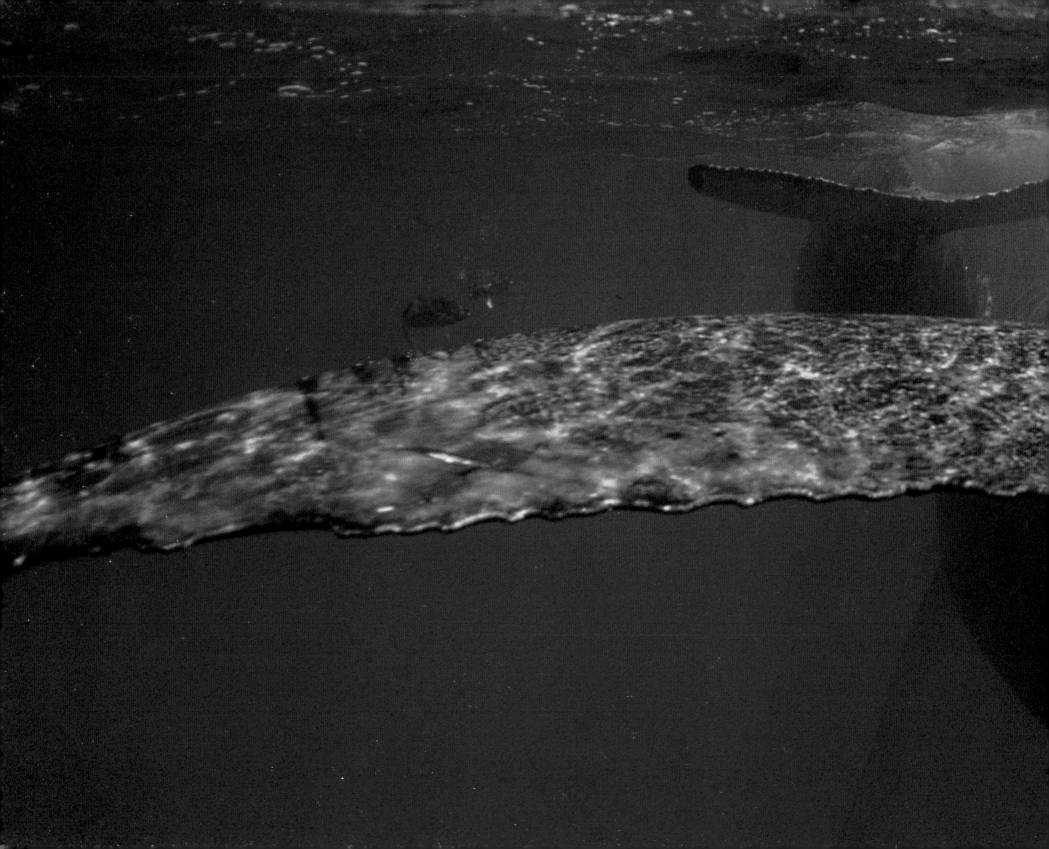

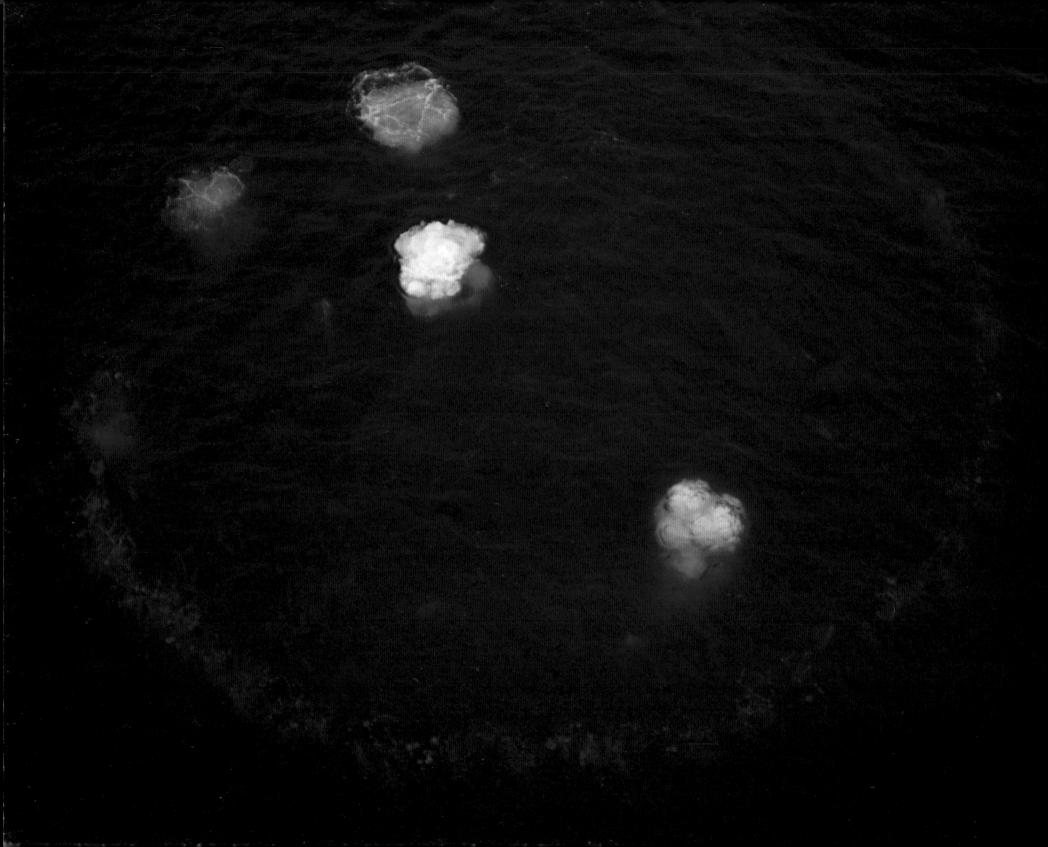

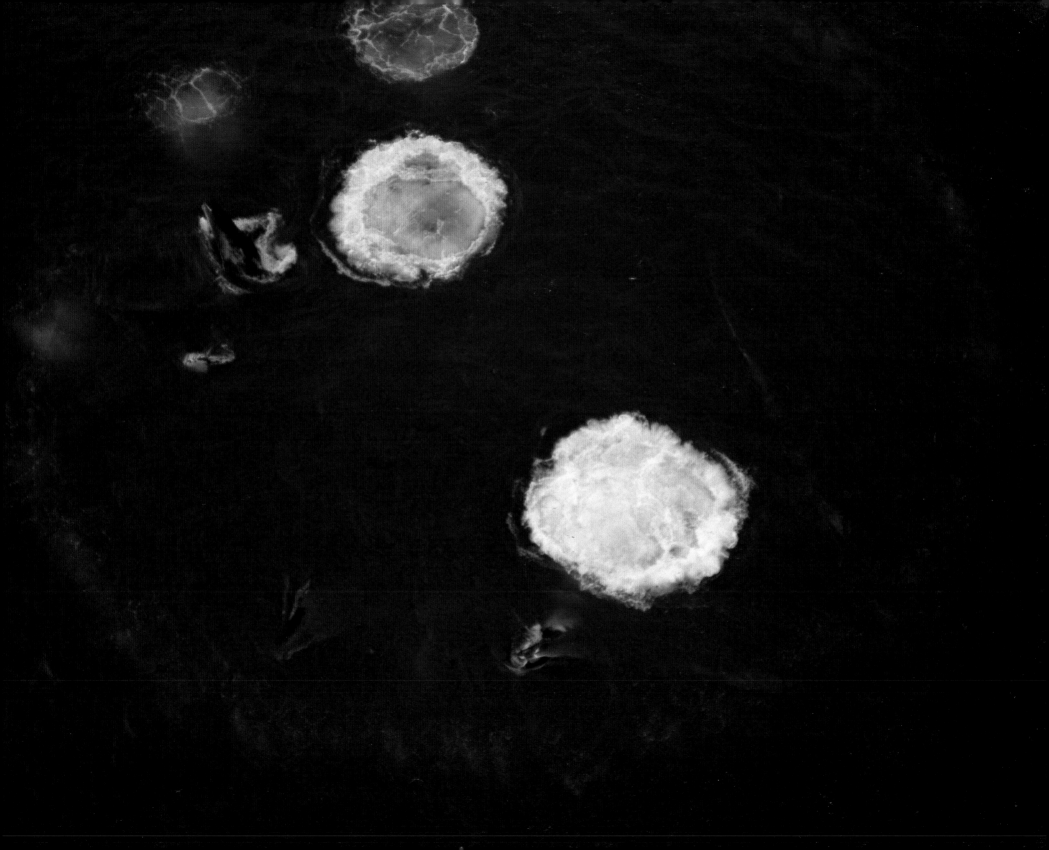

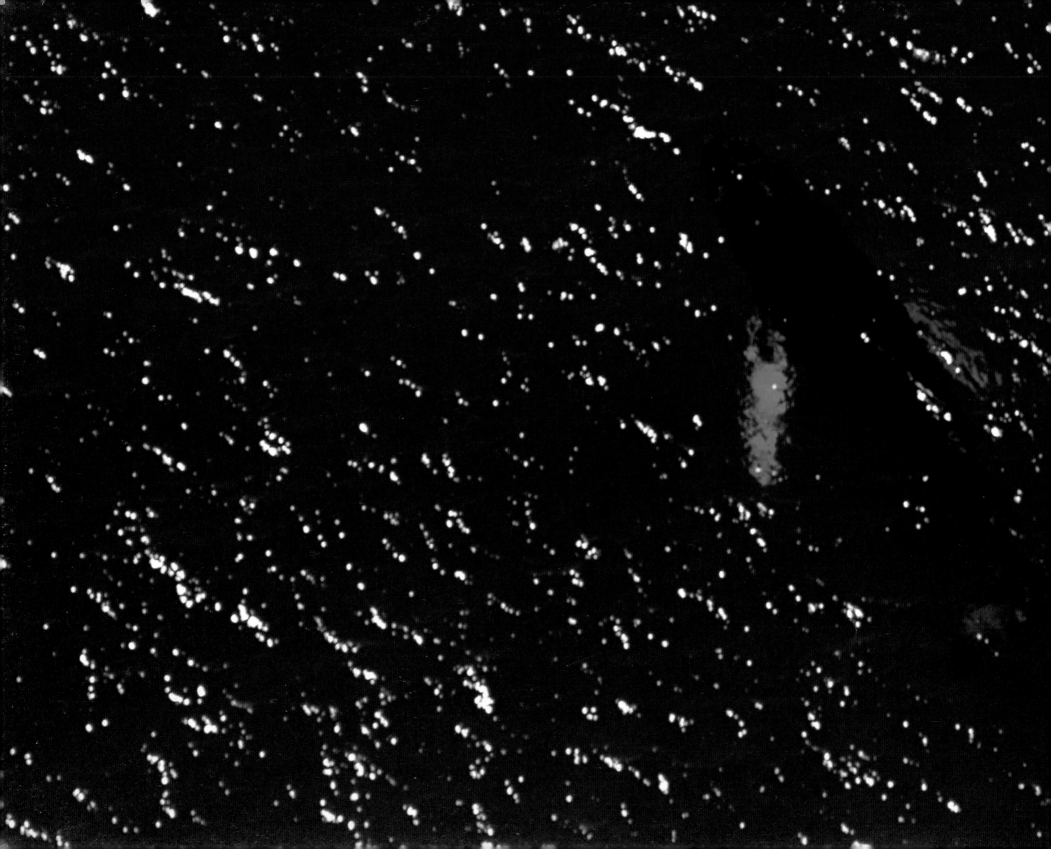

LET BEAUTY ABIDE

LEAVE THE DIVINE IN PEACE

Of Whales and the Sea

Whenever I see a whale, I am enthralled by its magical power. I feel this no less now than when I saw humpback whales for the first time in December, 1974, at the South Pole. As I stood at the bow of the boat, I sighted two of them swimming together. Slowly they approached the boat and spouted. Their thick, white spray floated in the air, then dispersed and clung softly to my cheeks and camera. In my intense excitement, I began to tremble. At that moment, beneath the South Pole's summer sun, I sensed I had been shown the infinite power of nature.

Since the impact of that encounter, I have sought out humpback whales around the world and have recorded my odyssey in words as well as images.

Hawaiian Islands, February, 1989.

It is eight o'clock in the morning, and I can hear humpback whales spouting over a hundred yards from my rubber raft. Their vapor rises as high as sixteen feet. Dorsal fins appear and disappear among the waves. I see another spout—a small one this time. The whale first sinks under the surface, and then bobs up thirty yards ahead of the raft.

After donning my face mask and fins, I silently slide into the luminous, transparent Hawaiian sea. The blue penetrates my body. Released from gravity, I sink into the water. I adjust my mask and blow through my snorkel—what a pitiful spout mine is!—then look around.

As I expected, the two humpbacks are an adult and a calf. In the distance, they look small, but their presence is certain. The variations in the ocean's blue strata seem to distort my sense of distance and my view of the creatures. I am near the surface, about a hundred feet diagonally above the whales. The young whale comes up. I wait quietly, feeling tense and nervous. I wonder if I am the first human being this young whale has ever encountered.

There is a popping sound as the juvenile takes a breath at the surface. Then, it sinks into the water and bounds upward, twists its flukes, and comes straight at me. Ten feet away, it cocks its head and looks at me.

I swim a bit with the little whale. I use a sidestroke, and so does the whale. I dive about fifteen feet, and so does the little whale. This child must think me one strange fellow.

Finally the mother whale swims up and takes her child away with her.

Chatham Strait, Southeastern Alaska, July, 1989.

I have been in a small rubber raft for ten hours. At ten o'clock at night, the wind is completely still, and the strait is calm. I stare intently at the surface of the water. This is summer in Alaska, so the chill crawls close and I feel it. The clouds break up, and a faint red light slants downward. It dully illuminates the quiet sea, turning the surface into a mirror.

I search for any bubbles rising from the ocean. I listen for sounds as if my entire body were an ear: small waves sloshing gently against my rubber raft, salmon leaping from the water, and, not far above me in the sky, the cries of gulls and bald eagles, echoing in the dark conifer forest on the shore.

Photographing whales is difficult. They do not appear at my convenience. Even if they appear, they might immediately submerge. Often by the time I find them and set up my camera, they have already gone. Opportunities come, but they last only an instant. Such are the demanding conditions under which I have to work. At times such as this evening, my intuition, experience, and patience are fully exercised. My frustration mounts.

Camera at the ready, afloat in my rubber raft, I wait to catch sight of humpback whales snaring their food, which they do through a kind of bubble-net feeding. Humpbacks swim in a tight circle while exhaling through their blowholes, creating a net of bubbles to enclose the schools of small fish that are their prey. The whales then swim upward toward the center of the circle, mouths open to gather the fish, and emerge in the circle of bubbles formed on the surface.

All day, I have been seeing the same behavior again and again, but I cannot get a good shot.

Once again, about thirty feet ahead of my raft, I see small bubbles start to burst on the surface, gradually followed by larger ones. The circles of bubbles form in a clockwise direction, expanding until they are about a hundred feet in diameter.

From within the circle comes a whooshing sound accompanied by a gurgling like that of a small stream. These two sounds suddenly stop, and a group of bubbles rises up, followed by a host of foot-long herring that flop around on the surface. The prey has been rounded up in the bubble net.

I await the whales. Where will they emerge from within their circular net? My nerves are stretched tight. I ready my camera again. The sea wells up and the surface seethes with foam. Three humpbacks emerge, their jaws agape. They scoop up their prey, filling their lower jaws with herring and seawater, then close their mouths and plunge back into the sea.

The humpbacks' feeding onset throws the sea into turmoil. The remaining fish scatter. Sea lions and Dall's porpoises gather after them. Black-legged kittiwakes swoop down from the sky, hoping for an evening meal.

Humpback whales spend the summer months feeding in the waters off Alaska. Come autumn and the breeding season, they migrate south to Hawaii, the place where they were born. When summer arrives again, they return north to Alaska.

This cycle has been repeated for countless years. The worldwide ban on the hunting of humpbacks, in force since 1966, ensures that the cycle will continue.

Mitsuaki Iwago

Whales are among the largest mammals on earth.

At five o'clock on a summer morning in Alaska, with a chill hanging in the air, the rising sun catches a spouting humpback.

The blast from the whale's spouting echoes resoundingly, and the vapor reaches some twenty feet.

The thick, white mist stays suspended in the chilly air for almost a minute.

A whale breathes by exhaling and inhaling through a blowhole at the top of its head.

In Frederick Sound, south of Admiralty Island, in southeast Alaska, a pod of six humpbacks picks up speed and heads north.

In this inner passage, among islands, channels, and a maze of intricate inlets, fish gather in abundance. The pod of six whales comes here to seek the riches of this northern sea.

A humpback over forty-five feet long and weighing some forty tons breaches, or leaps above the surface of the sea.

Twisting backward with a half spin through the air, the whale crashes onto its back.

A surfacing whale exposes the area from head to dorsal fin. Its blowhole sits on a slight bump on top of its head. Muscles usually keep the two nostrils tightly closed. By relaxing its muscles to open its nostrils, a whale can take in about nine hundred quarts of air per second.

Scattered around the head of a humpback are bumps ranging in size from a golf ball to a base-ball. Those on the upper and lower jaws have a small amount of body hair.

In early spring I saw this humpback breaching near Hahajima in the Bonin Islands off Japan. In winter the whales migrate from the north to the waters near these islands where they remain until the rough winter seas calm down toward the end of spring. Because female whales with their young have been spotted in this area, there is speculation that whales come here to reproduce.

The humpback's pectoral fin, longer than that of all other species of whales, is about one-third of its body length, from twelve to fifteen feet. This whale raised its fin high into the air and slowly hit against the water with a sharp, resounding smack. Slapping a pectoral fin may be a signal to other whales.

Here, a whale breaches in the waters off Alaska in the summer. After feeding, the whale energet-ically dances in the air. In the background can be seen an Alaskan coniferous forest and snow-capped peaks in Canada.

The pale inside of a pectoral fin, glaring in the bright sun, bears a pattern that differs from whale to whale.

During their summer in Alaska, humpbacks consume small fish, like herring and sardines. Each day one whale is able to devour an amount equivalent to about four percent of its forty ton mass. Tracking schools of small fish, a whale appears above the surface with its mouth wide open.

A humpback suddenly leaps from the water. It straightens out by stretching its upper body, then shifts its weight to plunge headfirst back into the water.

After scooping up fish, the whale closes its mouth. The area from the throat to the lower abdomen expands to accommodate seawater as well as fish. Clearly visible on the lower jaw and throat are barnacles and the marks left behind by their adhesion.

One of six whales heading north continuously raises and slams down its head. A nearby whale repeatedly slaps the water with its pectoral fins.

A humpback filters out seawater through its baleen, or whalebone, retaining the fish, then swallowing them. The baleen, resembling a long, thin, triangular strip of wood, grows along each side of the upper jaw.

The baleen grows from the roof of the mouth to the edges of the upper jaw. The outer baleen is smooth, but resilient and tough. The inner baleen has ragged strands that appear to give the whale a short thick beard.

A humpback that has spent all day eating performs a full breach against the background of the setting sun. Its flukes seem to dance above the ocean.

When a whale breaches, its left and right pectoral fins stretch from its sides. Maintaining its balance, the humpback bends backward and plunges into the sea.

A humpback exhales and falls onto its back against the backdrop of the Hawaiian island of Maui.

Why do whales breach? Perhaps they are trying to dislodge barnacles, whale lice, or remora. Or they are catching small fish by first stunning them. Or maybe whales are communicating. Or it could be that whales simply like to perform for an audience.

Breaching requires a great burst of energy. The whale flips its flukes up and down two or three times, then kicks, and flies into the air. It then topples thunderously, tossing up a flurry of spray.

A whale surfaces, takes a breath, and nosedives straight down halfway to the bottom of the roughly 250-foot-deep water.

The reproductive season for humpback whales lasts five months—from winter to the end of spring—and takes place in the Hawaiian Islands. After the females bear their young, they move to quiet, shallow water and wait for the calves to grow.

Swimming whales may look ponderous, but in fact travel fairly fast, at some eight knots per hour. A humpback gains momentum by using its waist as a fulcrum. The upward and downward motion of its flukes supplies the driving power. The movements of the left and right pectoral fins provide the steering.

A pectoral fin cuts through the water, tracing a curve of bubbles in its wake.

A humpback about two months old, swims toward me, twisting its body to the left, and lightly waving its flukes.

During the mating season, male humpbacks each sing a song consisting of several phrases and clearly possessing a melody with a wide range of tones. Singing his song, a male passes through a band of faint blue light.

High clear whistles and low moans are among the repertoire of sounds of a single whale. Their voices are believed to be created by the flow of air between the nasal cavity and the pharynx. Whales likely use their vocabulary to communicate with each other about mating and feeding. Here, a female groans plaintively as she rolls left, casting her gaze toward me.

Whales are capable of hearing across a wide range of frequencies. Sounds directly impact the whale's body and apparently resonate from the eardrum to the inner ear by a route differing from that of terrestrial mammals. Since visibility under the ocean is limited, whales may rely largely on sound to perceive their world.

When January arrives, juvenile whales in the seas off Hawaii begin swimming more actively. Busily flipping their flukes, they cruise alongside their mothers. The humpback gestation period is about twelve months, enough time for a female to journey from Hawaii to Alaska and back.

A young whale must rise to the surface every three to five minutes to breathe. Its mother is able to remain submerged for ten to fifteen minutes. So sometimes the mother stays below and watches her calf ascend to take its next breath.

Except for when they separate from each other to breathe, mother and young always swim together. I have seen a few juveniles with parts of their flukes missing. Young whales that swim away from their mothers are easy targets for sharks and other predators.

Mother and juvenile ascend to the surface to breathe. As they rise, the light penetrating the ocean makes them more distinct. Their huge shadow briefly falls over me then moves on.

When migrating humpbacks arrive in Hawaii, researchers begin their observations. Every day, in the water and from the land, they conduct their studies.

This researcher is photographing a female's reproductive organ and the pair of nipples on both sides of the organ. By studying the females, the researcher is trying to ascertain the social structure of a group of Hawaiian humpbacks.

In mid-afternoon, several humpback spouts rise over the surface of the slightly roughened sea. After securing my raft, I dive into the water and see an unusually large number of whales. A male rising toward the surface swims into my view, moving his pectoral fins up and down as he ascends.

I count eight humpbacks under the surface—a remarkably large female surrounded by seven whales, three females and four males swimming around her as if inscribing a sphere of about twenty feet in diameter.

Three of the seven separate from the group and snuggle against each other. They disperse, face each other again, arch gracefully backward, and then swim around together before returning to the group. Their staccato cries and high-pitched whines resonate throughout the water.

As the sun sets, the whiteness of the humpbacks' pectoral fins and flukes briefly stands out against the dark water. The eight whales become indistinguishable, then are gone.

A juvenile whale returning from a breathing run is passed by its mother on her way to the surface. The young whale follows her by vigorously waving its flukes.

Newborn whales are a pale gray color and ten to fifteen feet long, or about one-fourth the length of their mothers. The calves receive nourishment from their mothers' milk.

As whales adapted to their ocean habitat, they developed pectoral fins and flukes. The flukes, about fifteen feet wide, extend from the base of the backbone. The upward and downward motion of the flukes propels the whale forward.

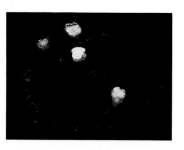

As humpbacks begin to feed, small, then large, bubbles appear on the surface of the water.

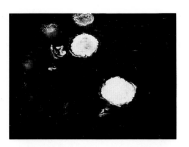

Feeding humpbacks swim in a circle while exhaling through their blowholes to create cylinder-shaped nets of fine bubbles that enclose schools of small fish.

The whales continue to feed into the evening. In Alaska in the summer, the sun sets after 10:30 at night.

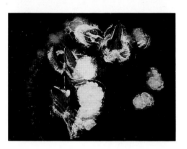

Humpbacks emerge from the water to swallow their prey. Occasionally, a humpback uses its pectoral fins to herd escaping fish into its open mouth.

In the Alaskan seas, convection currents carry underwater plankton up to the surface where it is consumed by small fish. Swimming through the green, plankton-rich water, the humpbacks search for schools of feeding fish.

The day's feeding concludes and a humpback heads toward a channel by kicking off with its flukes. The seas off Alaska still hold enough food to supply the whales during their four months in northern waters.

Nine humpbacks feed on herring. Each whale in turn scoops up the fish in its lower jaw, closes its mouth, and sinks back into the sea. A few minutes later, it reemerges, mouth wide open, to feed again.

After spouting six times, this whale flaps its flukes and submerges.

Every time I have seen a group of humpbacks feeding, the centermost whale seems to catch the most fish. I wonder if humpbacks have a leader on their hunting expeditions.

In a gesture called tail cocking, a whale flips its flukes on the surface to form a fan.

Individual humpback whales can be identified by the overall shape and white pattern on the undersides of their flukes. The patterns are like human fingerprints: each individual has a unique set. By following individual whales, researchers have tracked the species' migrations between Alaska and Hawaii and between Hawaii and Mexico.

A humpback raises its flukes, holding one of its pectoral fins out to one side for balance.

In tail slapping, a humpback turns over, looks upward, and slaps the water repeatedly with its upraised flukes.

A humpback displays aggression with a peduncle slap—a forceful whipping of the water.

A close-up view shows the massiveness and power of a humpback's flukes.

A whale returns underwater after taking a breath.

Scars along this whale's body suggest the dangers of life in the open sea.

Another whale rises to breathe, then reveals its impressive flukes.

This whale starts to do a tail slap, then makes a peduncle slap, perhaps protesting the presence of my rubber raft. After twisting its body, the whale crashes diagonally against the water.

Whales give each other peduncle slaps and sometimes aggressively bash each other.

In the Alaska twilight, a lone humpback spouts.

Twilight lingers for a long time during an Alaskan summer. This is at 9:30 in the evening.

As the sun sets, the temperature drops sharply. A humpback's flukes row against the sea. A spout rises in the air.

A juvenile, born in Hawaii, has migrated to Alaska. Occasionally, it moves a few hundred yards away from its mother. With its pectoral fin upraised, it seems to be bidding us farewell.

From a thousand feet up, we spot this humpback male off Maui Island singing his song. His singing continues for about twenty minutes as he heads southward.

In the sea around Hawaii, a mother and her young.

In Appreciation of the Sea

Mitsuaki Iwago

Born in Tokyo, Japan, in 1949, Mitsuaki Iwago has been involved with photography since he was a child. After graduating from college, he began to pursue a career in photography. Since that time, he has studied almost every area on earth. A keen observer of animal behavior, he has used his extensive knowledge in the pursuit of his photography. His beautiful and evocative photographs and feature articles have appeared in such prestigious publications as *National Geographic*. *Life* magazine selected him as one of the finest photographers of the 1980s. *Serengeti: Natural Order on the African Plain* (Chronicle Books, 1987), a collection of his photographs made during his stay in Africa's Serengeti National Park with his family from 1982 to 1984, has become a worldwide best-seller. Iwago began to produce a video series in 1989, which he continues with his program *Mitsuaki Iwago's Nature World*, in partnership with NHK.

Thanks to:

U.S. National Marine Fisheries Service, Pacific Whale Foundation, Greg Kaufman, Paul Forestell, Mike Osmond, Jan Straley, Jeff Jacobson, Charles Jurasz, NHK TV, Makoto Nagano, Tatsuo Kozaki, People of Ogasawara Village, Hideko Iwago.

Photographs of whales taken in United States waters were authorized by the National Marine Fisheries Service, under Research Permit 565 issued to the Pacific Whale Foundation.

First published in the United States in 1994 by Chronicle Books.

First published in Japan in 1990 by Shogakukan, Inc.

Printed in Singapore.

ISBN: 0-8118-0557-3 (PB)
ISBN: 0-8118-0585-9 (HC)

Library of Congress Cataloging-in-Publication Data available.

Cover and text design: Sarah Bolles
Book design: Keisuke Konishi
Cartography: Hiroyuki Kimura (TUBE)
Editing (Japanese edition): Shuji Shimamoto
Editing (American edition): Judith Dunham

Distributed in Canada by Raincoast Books
112 East Third Ave., Vancouver, B.C. V5T 1C8

10 9 8 7 6 5 4 3 2 1

Chronicle Books
275 Fifth Street
San Francisco, California 94103